My Very Own Octopus

My Very Own Octopus

by Bernard Most

Voyager Books
Harcourt Brace & Company
San Diego   New York   London

Voyager Books is a registered trademark of
Harcourt Brace & Company.

Library of Congress Cataloging-in-Publication Data
Most, Bernard.
My very own octopus.
"Voyager Books."
Summary: A boy imagines what fun he would have
with a pet octopus.
[1. Octopus—Fiction. 2. Pets—Fiction.]
1. Title.
PZ7.M8544My   1991
[E] 80-12786
ISBN 0-15-256345-8

Typography by Lori J. McThomas

L K J I H

Printed in Hong Kong

To Eric, for his love of marine life

*Also Written and Illustrated
by Bernard Most*

Hippopotamus Hunt
How Big Were the Dinosaurs?
Can You Find It?
Where to Look for a Dinosaur
Zoodles
Happy Holidaysaurus!
Pets in Trumpets and Other
    Word-Play Riddles
A Dinosaur Named after Me
The Cow That Went OINK
The Littlest Dinosaurs
Dinosaur Cousins?
Whatever Happened to the Dinosaurs?
If the Dinosaurs Came Back

I wish I had a pet of my own. I can't have a dog. I can't have a cat. I can't even have a rabbit since they make my brother sneeze.

But who ever heard of an *octopus* making anybody sneeze? I never did. I wish I had an octopus.

It would be easy to take an octopus home. My octopus could sit in the back with me.

My octopus and I could play baseball together. We'd be a whole team all by ourselves. Nobody would be able to hit the ball past us . . . not even my brother, Glenn, who is the best hitter of them all.

When we have dinner, my octopus could pass the salt and the pepper and the ketchup and the mustard whenever I needed them.

And, when we finished, my octopus could help my brother and me clear the table. Of course we would share our allowance with my octopus for helping us.

It would be great fun to take a bath with my octopus because we both love the water. I could have my back scrubbed and my hair washed all at the same time. And I would never have to worry about losing the soap!

When I go to sleep, my octopus could help me hug my animals — all at one time — and keep the covers from sliding off the bed.

I could take out
more books from
the library because
my octopus could
help me carry them
home.

My octopus would
like to read books,
too.

My octopus would come with me the next time we went to pick apples. I bet we could pick enough apples to last ten years.

On Halloween, my octopus could go around with me, and we would collect more treats than Glenn and all the other kids. People would wonder who my friend is with such a great costume.

In the winter, my octopus and I could beat anybody in a snowball fight . . . even my brother, Glenn, who is the best snowball maker of them all.

My octopus and I could shovel the driveway for my dad. Of course my dad would have to buy lots more shovels, but he wouldn't mind.

When I lose one of my mittens, which I always seem to do, my octopus would always have extra mittens for me to wear.

My room would always look neat because my octopus would help me put away all my clothes.

And when my friend David came to visit, my octopus would help us put away all my toys.

Sometimes my octopus and I would have a fight, like my brother and me. But it would be fun when we made friends again. We would shake

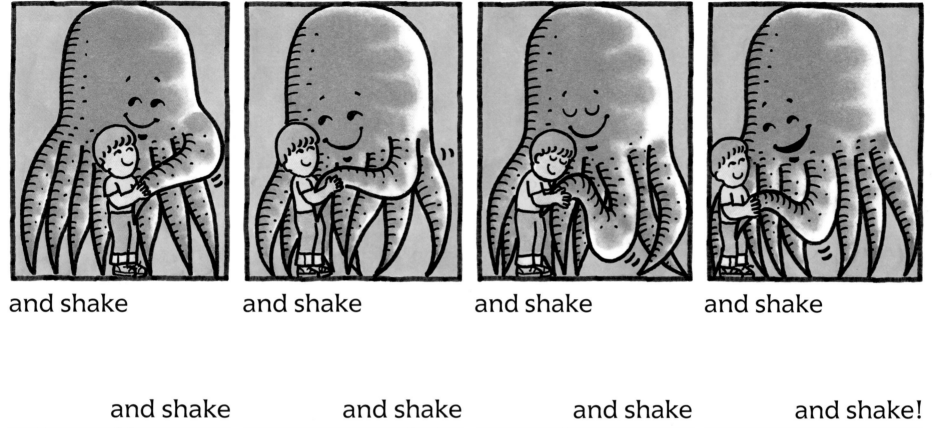

and shake   and shake   and shake   and shake

and shake   and shake   and shake   and shake!

We would always take my octopus to the store when we went shopping. Our cart would be filled in no time at all. And anything our cart couldn't hold, my octopus would.

I would never get wet again walking home from school in the rain. And neither would my brother nor any of my friends.

And the next time that big bully at school picks on me, my octopus would show him.

That big bully
would never pick
on me or my
friends again.

And whenever I fell and cried, or hurt myself, my octopus would always be there to help me up

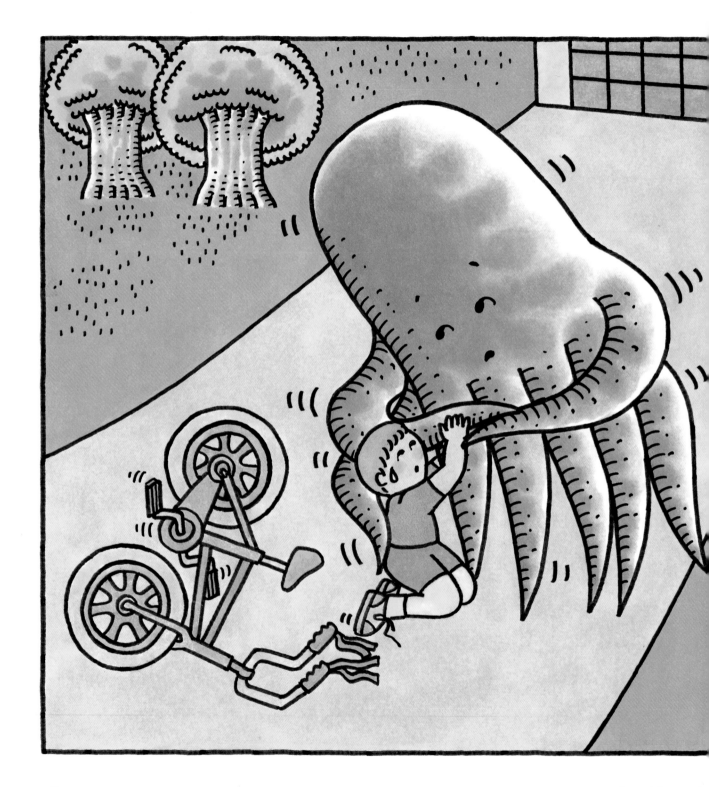

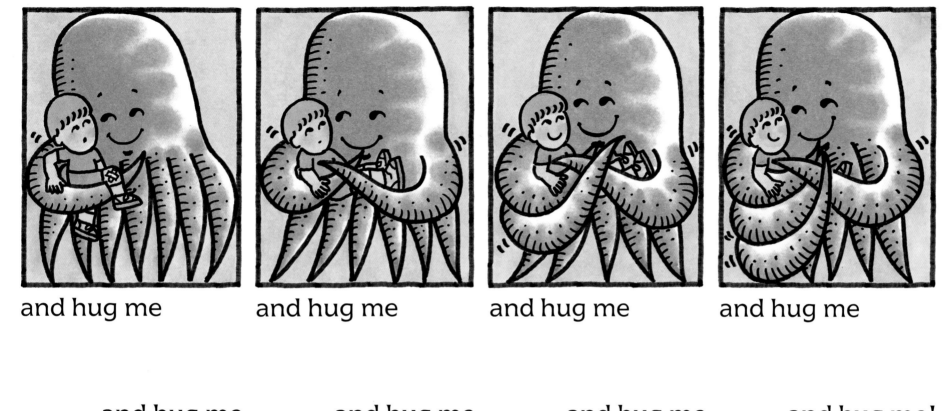

and hug me   and hug me   and hug me   and hug me

and hug me   and hug me   and hug me   and hug me!

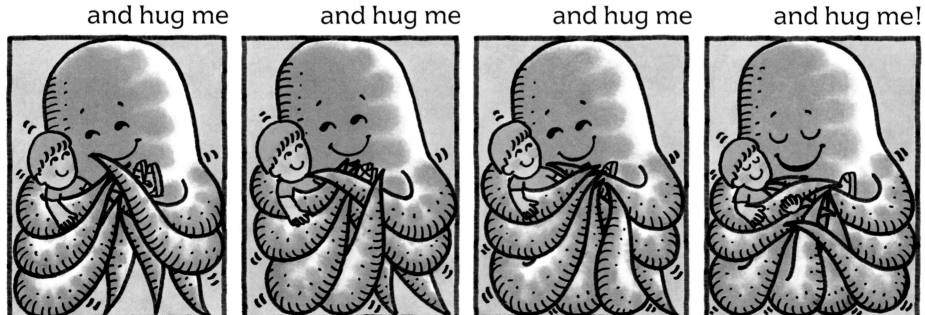

I wish I had my very own octopus.